Emily and Albert

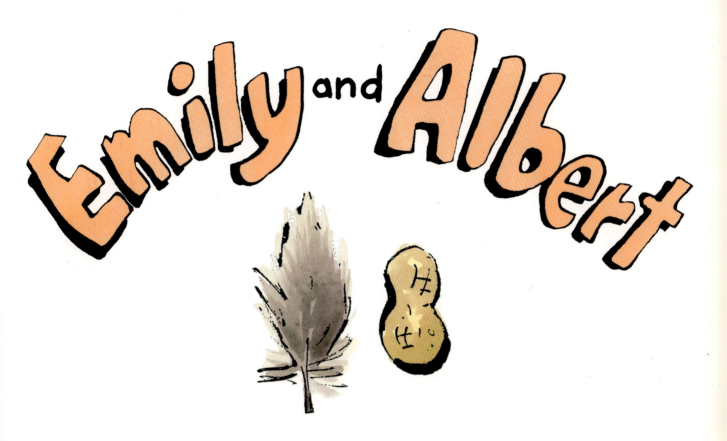

By Jan Ormerod

Illustrated by David Slonim

chronicle books · san francisco

Book design by Kristen M. Nobles.
Typeset in EideticNeo and Providence Sans.
The illustrations in this book were rendered in reed pen and ink and watercolors
on Arches 140-pound watercolor paper.
Manufactured in Hong Kong.

Library of Congress Cataloging-in-Publication Data
Ormerod, Jan.
Emily and Albert / by Jan Ormerod ; illustrated by David Slonim.
p. cm.
Summary: Emily the ostrich and Albert the elephant share a friendship in
which they compare noses, dance, read together, and more.
ISBN 0-8118-3615-0
[1. Friendship—Fiction. 2. Ostriches—Fiction.
3. Elephants—Fiction.] I. Slonim, David, ill. II. Title.
PZ7.O634Ej 2004
[E]—dc22
2003010806

Distributed in Canada by Raincoast Books
9050 Shaughnessy Street, Vancouver, British Columbia V6P 6E5

10 9 8 7 6 5 4 3 2 1

Chronicle Books LLC
85 Second Street, San Francisco, California 94105

www.chroniclekids.com

contents

For Susan Pearson—J. O.

To Brett and Debbie—D. S.

Chapter One

noses

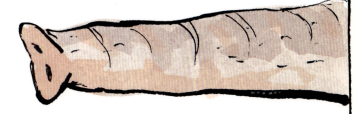

Emily and Albert are friends.

Emily has a little nose with ten tiny freckles.

Emily's nose is good for smelling things.

Albert has a long pink-and-gray trunk.

Albert's trunk is good for smelling things…

…and picking flowers
and finding lost buttons
and lifting Emily up
and carrying Emily's things.

Albert's trunk is good for making showers

and comforting a friend.

"Never mind," says Emily.

"We can't *all* have a little nose with freckles."

Chapter Two

hiccups

HIC!

Albert had the hiccups.

He drank a glass of water.

HIC!

Albert still had the hiccups.

He drank a glass of water
while he held his breath for a long time.

HIC!

Albert still had the hiccups.

He drank a glass of water
and held his breath for a long time
while he stood on his head.

HIC!

Albert still had the hiccups.

Along came Emily.

"Hello, Albert," said Emily.

HIC!

"I have the hiccups," said Albert.

"You have the hiccups, Albert," said Emily.

"You need to drink a glass of water
while you hold your breath for a long time
and stand on your head."

Albert drank a glass of water
while he held his breath for a long time
and stood on his head again.
The hiccups went away.

"Simple," said Emily.

"Easy-peasy," said Albert.

Chapter Three

dancing

Albert loves to mambo.

Emily loves ballet.

Albert loves to tango.

Emily loves ballet.

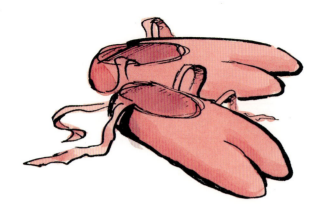

Albert loves to rhumba and salsa.

Emily loves ballet.

Albert loves to cha-cha and fox-trot.

Emily loves ballet.

"You are a very good ballet dancer, Albert," said Emily.

"Thank you," said Albert.

Chapter Four

"You look sick, Albert," said Emily.

"I don't feel sick," said Albert.

"You shouldn't sit in a draft," said Emily.

She wrapped Albert up warm.

She took his temperature.

"I need lunch," said Albert.

"You're too sick for lunch," said Emily.

She put a cool cloth on his forehead.

"I need to ride my bike," said Albert.

"You need your rest," said Emily.

She rubbed smelly stuff on his chest.

She tucked him into bed.

When Emily went out to play,

Albert got out of bed.

He took off the hot scarf.

He ate a hearty lunch of cheese-and-pickle sandwiches,

bananas, pineapple pieces, and custard in a little pot.

Then he went for a long bike ride.

He got home just before Emily.

"Albert," cried Emily, "you are well again.

I made you well again."

"Yes," said Albert. "You are a good doctor, Emily."

Chapter Five

a good book

Albert was snuggled up under his quilt.

"You wouldn't be cold if you were doing something,"

said Emily.

"I'm not cold," said Albert.

"I'm reading a good book."

"I don't just read about things," said Emily.

"I *do* things."

"I *am* doing something," said Albert.

"I am reading a really good book."

"I don't think it can be a *good* book

if it makes others feel lonely

while you are reading it," said Emily.

"Would you like me to read you a story from my book?"

said Albert.

"Could I snuggle up under your quilt?" said Emily.

"Certainly," said Albert.

"With a peanut-butter sandwich?" said Emily.

"Of course," said Albert.

"This is a *really* good book," said Emily.

"Glad you like it," said Albert.